Blue's
Big
Birthday

**To my husband, Gregory,
who always helped to make
my dreams come true—A. C. S.**

Loving thanks to the Sweet Little Mowen Child—T. P. J.

To my mother and father, and to Jeannie and Ellen, for all their love and support—S. K. K.

Based on the TV series *Blue's Clues*™ created by Traci Paige Johnson, Todd Kessler, and Angela C. Santomero as seen on Nick Jr.® On *Blue's Clues,* Steve is played by Steven Burns.

SIMON SPOTLIGHT
An imprint of Simon & Schuster Children's Publishing Division
1230 Avenue of the Americas, New York, New York 10020

Manufactured in the United States of America
First Edition 10 9 8 7 6 5 4
ISBN 0-689-85103-0

Blue's Big Birthday

By Angela C. Santomero

Illustrated by
Traci Paige Johnson and
Soo Kyung Kim

Simon Spotlight/Nick Jr.

New York London Toronto Sydney Singapore

It's Blue's birthday! Thank you so much for coming early to the party. We could sure use your help getting everything ready. Will you help us?

Blue, what do you really, really want for your birthday?

Oh! Blue's Clues! We are going to play Blue's Clues! Do you know how to play? Great! Blue's pawprints will be on three clues, and the clues will tell us what she really wants for her birthday!

Now we need to clean up this pawprint . . . but how?
Will you blow the pawprint away and then turn the page really fast? Ready? One, two, three, GO!

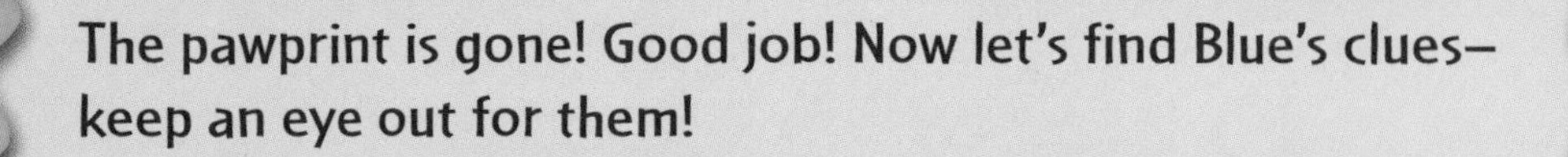
The pawprint is gone! Good job! Now let's find Blue's clues–
keep an eye out for them!

Our first clue! And it's the color . . . do you know what color this is?
Green! We need to write down this clue in our handy-dandy notebook!

Will you help us bake our special cake for Blue's birthday? This is the recipe.

HAPPY BIRTHDAY

1 2 ½

How many blueberries do we need? How many eggs?

How much milk do we need?

Do you want to help? Look around the kitchen and try to find all of the things we need for Blue's special cake.

Hey, look at that! You found all of the ingredients!
Mr. Salt and Mrs. Pepper are mixing them up!
Mixa, mixa, mixa. Poura, poura, poura. Baka, baka, baka–
Blue's birthday cake!

We'll check on Blue's birthday cake later. Did you find our second clue? Me too! I put it in my handy-dandy notebook already! Let's set the party table now, okay? We'll need ten of everything, since there will be ten of us at the party. Will you help me count ten spoons and bring them outside? You will? Thanks!

Thank you for bringing out all ten spoons! You are a really good counter! I set the party table for all of our guests. Would you check the table and see if I forgot anything? Oh! I think one of our balloons is missing. And a star lantern, too! Do you know which ones?

You were really good at finding those missing things. We put some more birthday decorations around too. Do you see what we've added? Oh! We found our third clue! A shell! You know what that means: We are ready for our . . . thinking chair! Let's go!

Do you remember what our three clues were? The color green, a fish tank, and a shell. So, what could Blue want for her birthday that is the color green, can be in a fish tank, and lives in a shell?

Blue wants a **turtle** for her birthday! That's the answer to Blue's Clues, because . . . most turtles are the color green . . . and can be in a fish tank . . . and live in a shell! We just figured out Blue's Clues!

Dingdong. That's the doorbell! The rest of our party guests must be here! Let's go have Blue's birthday party!

I'm so excited! I just love birthdays! Do you know all of Blue's friends who came to the party? Can you guess which friend gave Blue which present? Do you see the special birthday cake we helped Mr. Salt and Mrs. Pepper make?

Thank you so much for coming and helping with the party.

You made Blue's day special!